BRICK BY BRICK

Heidi Woodward Sheffield

Nancy Paulsen Books

To Mom and Dad,
who built their lives
brick by brick

Nancy Paulsen Books
An imprint of Penguin Random House LLC, New York

Visit us online at penguinrandomhouse.com

Library of Congress Cataloging-in-Publication Data
Names: Sheffield, Heidi Woodward, author. | Title: Brick by brick / Heidi Woodward Sheffield.
Description: New York: Nancy Paulsen Books, [2020] | Summary: As a little boy watches his father, a bricklayer, work hard to build the city, both dream of building a house of their own.
Identifiers: LCCN 2019018193 | ISBN 9780525517306 (hardcover: alk. paper) |
ISBN 9780525517320 (ebook) | ISBN 9780525517313 (ebook)
Subjects: | CYAC: Bricklaying—Fiction. | Fathers and sons—Fiction. |
Building—Fiction. | House construction—Fiction. | Hispanic Americans—Fiction.
Classification: LCC PZ7.1.S5114 Bri 2020 | DDC [E]—dc23
LC record available at https://lccn.loc.gov/2019018193
Manufactured in China by RR Donnelley Asia Printing Solutions Ltd.
ISBN 9780525517306
10 9 8 7 6 5 4 3 2 1

Design by Semadar Megged and Nicole Rheingans | Text set in Coventry ITC Std
The illustrations were created using photographs, digital painting, and collage.
Heidi used brick photos to create Papi and Luis, emphasizing their strength and fortitude.
Antique lace, embroidery, and textile images courtesy of The Lace Museum Detroit.
Image from *Design Motifs of Ancient Mexico* courtesy of Dover Publications, Inc.
Images from *361 Full-Color Allover Patterns* courtesy of Dover Publications, Inc.
Images from *Flowers* courtesy of Dover Publications, Inc.

Mi papi es fuerte—
my papi is strong.

He's a bricklayer.
His arms are like stone.

When Papi builds,
he spreads the mortar thick.
TAP TAPS the brick in place.
SCRRRRAPES the drips.
Starts again.

He helps build the city, brick by brick.

At work, Papi climbs the scaffold
and touches the sky.
Papi is not afraid of heights.

Me neither.
At recess, I touch the sky, too.

DOG TRAINING

Raising Fido

Puppy Tales

Happy Dogs

Papi's work is
brick
by brick.

Mine is
book
by book.

I dream of a house for us.
Nuestra casa para siempre—
our always house—
with a garden for Mama
and maybe a dog for me.

"When, Papi?"
"Someday," he says.

At lunch, Papi whistles,
eats Mama's special empanada,
drinks cinnamon horchata,
KERCHUNKS his lunch box closed.

I do, too.

Then it's back to work again.
Papi makes the mortar
that hold the bricks together.
He turns on the mixer,
WHIRRRRRRR,
pours the water,
WHOOSH.
He shovels sand and
adds cement.

I roll my clay,
SLAP and PAT.
I pinch and smooth and
mold it.

I make a tiny dog and tiny
bricks for a tiny house.

When the sunlight
starts to fade,
dusty Papi picks me up.
He is tired, but smiling.

Papi feels like the sun,
hot and glistening.

Saturday is our special day.
Papi cooks me a yummy breakfast.
He lets me try his big hat on.

"Close your eyes," Papi says.
"Una sorpresa. A surprise."

We ride away in his
rumbling truck.

The road is rough,
BUMP BUMP.
I want to sneak a peek,
but I don't.

After a while, we stop.

"¡SORPRESA!" Papi yells.

It's a new house
made of
Papi's bricks!

Tonight I dream
in my house.
Nuestra casa
para siempre—
our always house.

And when spring comes,
I help Mama plant our flowers.